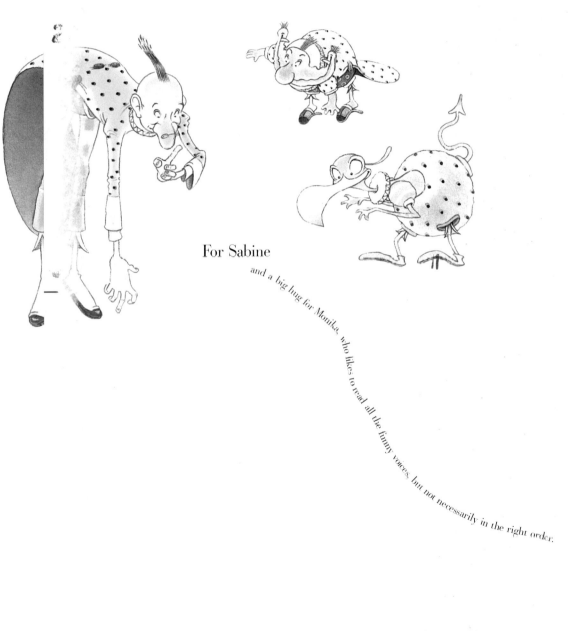

For Sabine

and a big hug for Monika, who likes to read all the funny voices, but not necessarily in the right order.

TITLE:

THE GHOST LIBRARY

AUTHOR: by David Melling

British Library Cataloguing in Publication Data
A catalogue record of this book is available from
the British Library.

ISBN 0 340 86088 X (HB)
ISBN 0 340 86089 8 (PB)
Copyright © David Melling 2004
The right of David Melling to be identified as the author
and illustrator of this Work has been asserted by him in
accordance with the Copyright, Designs and Patents Act 1988.
First edition published 2004
This paperback edition published 2005
10 9 8 7 6 5 4 3 2 1
Published by Hodder Children's Books, a division of
Hodder Headline Limited, 338 Euston Road, London NW1 3BH
Printed in China

THIS BOOK IS THE PROPERTY OF THE GHOST LIBRARY.
IT MUST BE RETURNED BEFORE MIDNIGHT.

THE GHOST LIBRARY

DAVID MELLING

Hodder
Children's
Books

A division of Hodder Headline Limited

Bo had gone to bed early. She wasn't tired so she decided to read her favourite book. The story was great – it was about a witch who had smelly feet.

And Bo had just got to the interesting part about strawberry-flavoured socks, when without warning…

...the lights went out!

Bo felt a cold chill.

Whispers sniffled
and snuffled in
the dark.

I can't see a thing!

It's here somewhere!

'Ow,
that's my
nose!'

Shadows
shivered
closer.

A clammy hand grabbed Bo's book.

It was so sudden and Bo was holding it so tightly

that the book and Bo were jerked into the air!

'GOT IT!' squealed a voice.

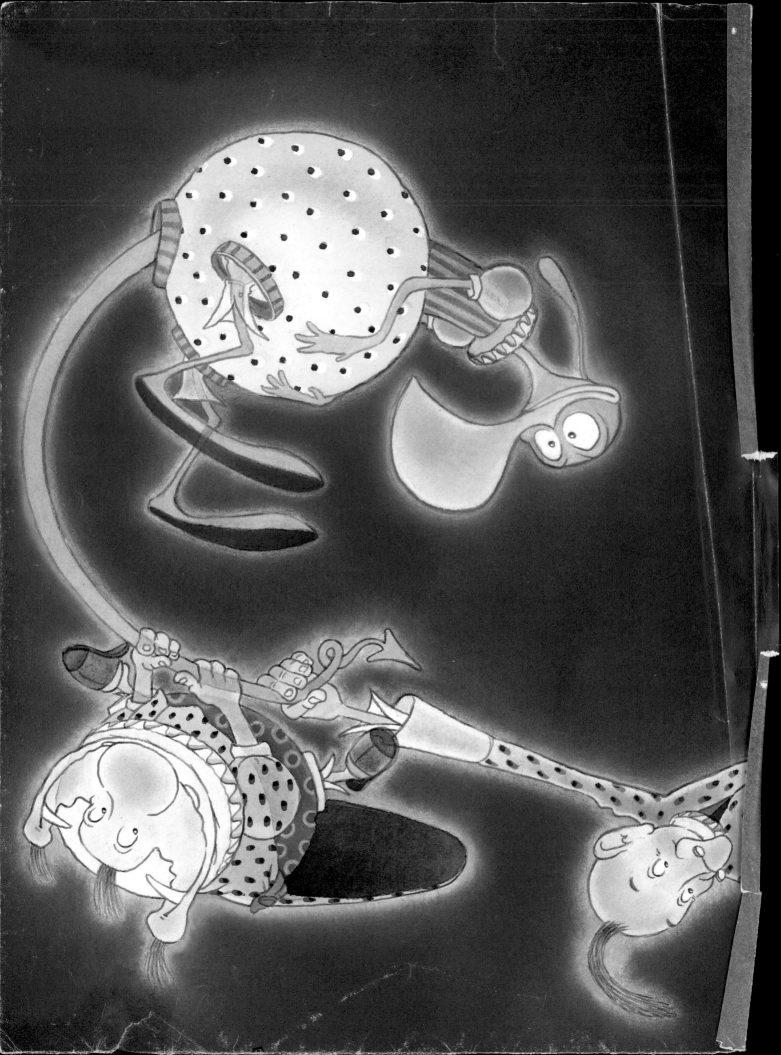

Bo kept her eyes shut and tried not to let go.

So she didn't see how she passed through her bedroom wall, into the night sky and towards a very tall tower which hadn't been there five minutes ago!

Before she knew it, Bo found herself in...

'I must be dreaming,' thought Bo. She had never met any ghosts before, but she had always imagined that if she ever did, they would look very different to the three smiling at her now!

'Errr, hello,' said the tall one. 'I'm Magpie.'

'I'm Twit,' said another, floating round her head.

'And I'm Puddle Mud,' said a third voice from somewhere near her slippers. 'What a surprise. Welcome to The Ghost Library.'

'What do you mean "surprise"?' said Bo.
'You brought me here.'

'Um, yes,' said Magpie, looking a little uncomfortable.
'The thing is, we wanted your book, but you wouldn't
let go. So you… came with it.' He gave the book in Bo's
hand another little tug.

'We collect books for our library,' said Twit.

Bo looked up at the shelves. 'But it's completely empty!'

'You tried to steal my book,' said Bo crossly.

'Oh no,' spluttered Puddle Mud. 'We're not thieves. Only we don't have our own books, so we take children's books, read them a few times, then... we give them back!'

They looked sad and Magpie honked noisily into a tissue.

'Let's have a story,' said Twit quickly. They all looked at Bo.

'You want me to read you a story?' she said.

'Well, now that you're here, that would be lovely!' they said.

STORY TIME? yelped Twit.

All at once, Bo felt a terrible draught, as ghost after ghost flew into the library and popped out of the shelves.

As soon as they saw her the ghosts started chattering excitedly.

'Goodness, who's that?'

'I don't know, but I hope it's a good story!'

Eventually the murmuring stopped and it became very quiet. They waited.

Bo sighed. She sat down and began to read her book about the witch.

'In a dark and gloomy cave lived a witch, whose terrible feet were so stinky that her cat wore a clothes peg on its nose.
This made it very difficult to purr...'

'...and so, as long as she kept her boots on forever, she never smelt her feet again!'

Bo closed the book.

The ghosts were spellbound.

'Wow, that was a great story!' they said. 'Tell us another.'

'No,' said Bo. 'Now it's your turn. Why don't you tell me a story.'

'Oh we couldn't possibly,' they blushed.

'We don't know any,' said Magpie.

'That's why we borrow books. We're the Story Book Collectors.'

'But you can make up any story you like. Just look around you, they're everywhere!' said Bo.

Twit looked in his pockets. Then he took a peek in Puddle Mud's. They all started looking.

'No, not like that,' laughed Bo. 'I'll help you. Let's swap ideas.'

The ghosts were so excited they all shouted their ideas at once.

'There must be ghosts in it that make loud jibbery noises!'

'And sneaky creepy shadows!'

'With squinty eyes and spider-breath!'

'Of course!' cried Bo. 'Let's tell
A GHOST STORY!'

The ghosts decided that Bo was the best at
reading stories because she put funny voices in all
the right places. So they settled down and listened
to her read their story:

*'One damp and spooky night, three Story Book Collectors
crept into the bedroom of a little girl called Bo...'*

'...and to this day The Ghost Library is full of stories.

They're mostly about ghosts, but if you look
hard enough, you can find one about a witch,
a cat and a clothes peg.'

When Bo returned to her room she found a small card on her pillow.

On it were little silver letters that danced and glowed as she read…

FRIENDS OF THE GHOST LIBRARY

FULL MEMBERSHIP

And now, sometimes Bo visits The Ghost Library, and sometimes the ghosts visit her!

Whichever it is, they always insist that she reads to them… with all the funny voices in all the right places!